Bluebell Woods

Florence's River Adventure

For Robin, with lots of love XX
L.N.

i Tadcu, gyda chariad,
Rebecca XXX

STRIPES PUBLISHING
An imprint of Magi Publications
1 The Coda Centre, 189 Munster Road,
London SW6 6AW

A paperback original
First published in Great Britain in 2012

ISBN: 978-1-84715-225-1

Printed and bound in China.

STP/1800/0013/1211

10 9 8 7 6 5 4 3 2 1

Bluebell Woods

Florence's River Adventure

Liss Norton

Illustrated by Rebecca Harry

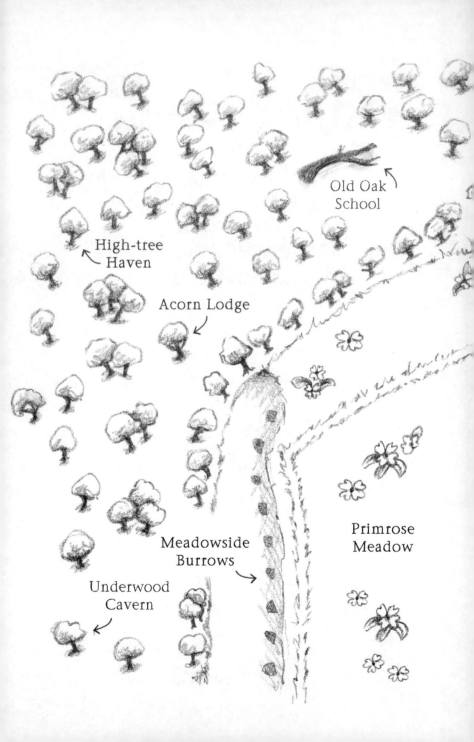

Old Oak
School

High-tree
Haven

Acorn Lodge

Meadowside
Burrows

Underwood
Cavern

Primrose
Meadow

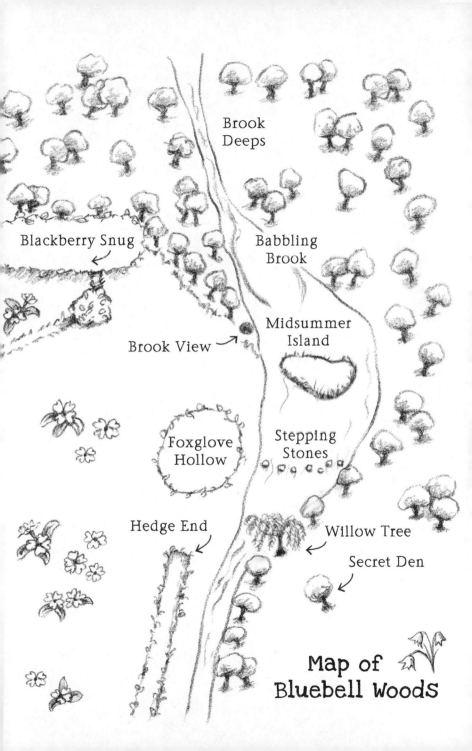

Brook
Deeps

Blackberry Snug

Babbling
Brook

Brook View

Midsummer
Island

Foxglove
Hollow

Stepping
Stones

Hedge End

Willow Tree

Secret Den

Map of
Bluebell Woods

Chapter One

Florence Candytuft was playing her new rosewood flute in her bedroom when her little sister came in. "I want the flute," she said, holding out a tiny paw.

"Not now, Rosie," said Florence, ruffling the silky fur on her head.

Rosie's ears drooped miserably. "Please," she quavered.

Florence sighed. The flute had been her birthday present from her mum and dad three days ago, but she'd hardly had the chance to play it at all. She'd asked for a flute because Mr Wintergreen, one of the Bluebell Woods musicians, had set up a school band at the beginning of the spring term and Florence had been eager to join. He'd said they had to practise hard, but that wasn't easy with Rosie around. She loved the flute just as much as Florence did.

"You can have it in a moment, when my friends get here," said Florence, trying not to look at Rosie's sad face.

Just then, she heard a knock at the front door of her burrow, and footsteps came scampering along the hall. Her friends Honey Pennyroyal, a wood mouse, Natalie Hollyhock, a hedgehog, and Evie Morningdew, a squirrel, burst into her room.

"Is that your birthday flute, Florence?" Evie asked admiringly, her eyes shining.

Florence held it up to show them. "Yes, isn't it lovely?"

"My flute," cried Rosie, reaching for it.

Florence sighed and handed it to her. "Go on then."

Tooting happily, Rosie hurried out of the room.

"She's so sweet," said Natalie.

"She is sweet," agreed Florence. "But trying to practise for the band with her about is a nightmare. She's flute-mad!"

She glanced out of the window and wrinkled her nose in disappointment. The morning had been wet and windy, and although the rain had finally stopped, the sky was still grey and the branches of the crab-apple tree near her burrow were still dripping. "I suppose my birthday picnic's off," she said. "The ground must be far too wet for picnics."

"Primrose Meadow's off, yes," Honey said, plonking herself down on Florence's bed. "But we thought we could eat in the den instead."

"And have your proper birthday picnic next Sunday," added Natalie.

"That way I'll get two birthday picnics," Florence said delightedly.

"If the rain's stopped by next week," said Evie. "Though I'm beginning to think the sun might never come out again! It doesn't feel much like spring."

"I'll touch my tail for luck!" Florence said. She led the way into the kitchen. Evie's picnic basket, which they were all sharing, sat on the table.

"I've already put in the pasties and cakes, darling," Mum said.

"Are they *carrot* pasties, Mrs Candytuft?" asked Honey hopefully, licking her lips.

"Yes, Honey. And caraway cakes."

"Yummy!" whooped Honey.

"Thanks, Mum," said Florence, giving her a kiss.

"Remember your hat," said her mum. She handed Florence a pretty straw hat decorated with purple ribbons and two small, white feathers.

"That really suits you," said Natalie, as Florence put it on. "Did you get it for your birthday?"

Florence nodded. "From Granny and Grandpa Applewood."

"Shame it's not pink," said Honey. "But it's still nice."

Florence laughed. "Come on," she said. "Let's go before it starts raining again."

Giggling, they ran out of the burrow and across Primrose Meadow, scattering the raindrops that clung to the arching stems of tall grasses.

Florence held on tight to her hat so it wouldn't blow away. Evie and Natalie carried the picnic basket between them.

Bluebell Woods

As they neared Honey's nest, Hedge End, they heard a loud banging and crashing.

"What's that?" cried Natalie, looking round in alarm.

"Harvey and Albie," groaned Honey. They were her twin brothers. "They're practising their drumming for the school band." She covered her ears. "What a racket!"

They ran on, glad to leave the din behind, then skirted Foxglove Hollow where the tall foxglove buds were already showing tinges of pinky-white. Scented violets grew here, too, their velvety, purple petals gleaming.

Soon they reached the Stepping Stones that crossed the Babbling Brook. On the far side, they could see a blue haze

under the trees – the bluebells that gave
the wood its name were already in flower.

"Me first!" Honey cried, springing
daintily on to the first Stepping Stone.
Florence followed her, letting go of her
hat and holding out her arms to balance.

Suddenly, a gust of wind whirled her
hat away, the ribbons flapping wildly.
"Catch it!" Florence cried, as it flew
towards Evie and Natalie, who were still
on the bank.

Dropping the picnic basket, they jumped for the hat, but the wind swept it back across the Babbling Brook to the opposite side.

"Come on!" shrieked Honey. She raced across the last few Stepping Stones with Florence close behind. Evie and Natalie grabbed the basket and charged after them.

The hat had come to rest on a dock leaf, but the wind whisked it away again before Florence could grab it. "Bother!" she cried.

The four friends pelted along the bank of the brook, the hat dancing ahead of them. From time to time, the wind let it settle, but whirled it away again as soon as they came close.

"The wind's playing a game with us," puffed Natalie.

"I just hope we win," cried Florence.

Granny and Grandpa had made the hat especially for her and brought it all the way from Bramble Bank, their village upstream.

On and on they ran until suddenly the hat plopped right into the middle of the Babbling Brook.

"How are we going to reach it now?" Evie groaned.

"I'll see if I can find a stick," Florence said. A tall weeping willow tree grew on the bank, the branches dangling in the water; perhaps there'd be a stick underneath the tree. Parting the leaves, she ducked under them, then stopped in surprise. Something was hidden among the reeds.

Heart thumping, she stretched up on tiptoe. "Quick!" she cried excitedly. "Come and see what I've found!"

Chapter Two

Honey, Natalie and Evie crawled in under the willow tree.

"Look!" exclaimed Florence. In the shallow water close to the bank, caught in the tree's roots and surrounded by reeds, was a small boat.

They crowded round. "Where do you think it came from?" asked Honey.

"Maybe someone dumped it," said Evie. "Or it might have blown away in a storm. The weather's been awful for the last couple of weeks."

Leaning forward, Florence parted the reeds so she could see better. "It must have been here a while," she said. "The reeds have grown up all round it."

"We could fix it up and go sailing!" said Evie.

Natalie frowned. "The boat doesn't belong to us, Evie."

"It doesn't seem to belong to *anyone*," Florence pointed out. "Nobody would want it in *that* state." The boat's paint had almost peeled off and the mast leaned to one side. A spider had spun a web from the top and a few dried willow leaves hung there.

"But we can't just take it," Natalie said, "even if it does look old and battered. What if the owner turns up?"

"If they wanted it they wouldn't leave it here to rot away in the reeds," said Evie.

Bluebell Woods

"Why don't we mend it and then see if we can track down the owner?" suggested Honey. "They'll probably be pleased to have their boat repaired."

"We could go out for just one sail," said Florence, "and then look for the owner. What do you think, Nat?"

"I suppose there's no harm in that," said Natalie thoughtfully.

"Brilliant!" Florence cheered. "Let's start work now." She flattened the reeds ahead of her with her front paws, then stepped on to them cautiously, testing them with her weight. To her relief, they didn't give way and plunge her into the water below. She was a strong swimmer, but it was nowhere near warm enough for a dip in the brook this early in the year.

"There's some cloth on the seat," she told her friends. She shook off the scattering of leaves. "Do you think it could be a sail?"

"Let's see, Florence!" cried Honey eagerly.

Florence handed it to her and she and Evie spread it out.

"It *is* a sail!" Natalie exclaimed. She looked it over carefully. "There's only one hole. I'm sure we can soon patch that up."

"Hurray!" cheered Honey, skipping round in a circle. "We'll be sailing in no time!"

"Let's see if we can pull the boat out of the reeds," Florence said, taking another step forward. Now she could see that there was water in the bottom of the boat. "Can someone pass me a mug from the picnic basket?" she asked. "So I can bail the boat out and make it a bit lighter."

They all came to help. "Yuck!" complained Honey. "The ground's all muddy and squelchy."

"Stand over here on the reeds then," said Florence.

It only took a few minutes to empty most of the water from the boat. "We should be able to get it out of the reeds and up on to the bank now," said Natalie.

"Hang about," said Evie. She bit off a long, bendy willow shoot, then threaded it through an iron ring fixed to the front of the boat. "This will make pulling easier," she said, giving one end to Natalie and gripping the other tightly.

Honey stood on one side of the boat, holding the plank seat, ready to push.

Florence headed round behind the boat, trampling a path through the reeds as she went. "Ready, steady, go!" she cried.

With Florence and Honey pushing and Evie and Natalie pulling, the boat moved a little, then stuck fast in the mud.

"It's not going to work," Honey wailed.

"Yes, it is!" Florence said determinedly. She pushed harder than ever and, all at once, the boat slid forward.

"One more push," gasped Evie.

Bending almost double, Florence threw all her weight behind the boat. Slowly it inched across the reeds, then up on to the bank. "At last!" she panted.

They all stood back to inspect the boat, their eyes wide with excitement. Now it was out of the water they could see that it badly needed painting, but the wood looked solid enough.

"The oars seem OK," said Evie, examining them.

"So do the seats," said Natalie. There were three plank seats, a narrow one at either end and a wider one across the middle that was big enough for two.

"And look at the mast," Honey said. "It's not broken. It's only come out of the socket."

"We'll have to paint the boat," Florence said. "I wonder what colour…"

"Let's paint it pink," suggested Honey. "That will look lovely!"

Natalie peeled off a flake of paint. "It was red before, if this bit of paint's anything to go by."

"We should go for red then," Florence said. "Just in case we find the owner." She hoped they wouldn't. She couldn't imagine anything nicer than sailing along the Babbling Brook on a sunny day.

Suddenly, her paw flew to her mouth. "I've forgotten my hat!" she gasped. Darting out from under the willow tree, she scanned the brook, but her hat had vanished. "I suppose it's sunk," she said glumly.

Natalie squeezed her paw. "What a shame!"

"It can't be helped," said Florence. "I should have held on to it properly."

"Not more rain!" exclaimed Honey, as a large water drop landed on her nose. "Just when we want to start fixing the boat. Typical!"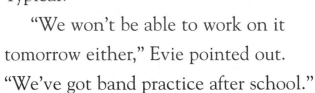

"We won't be able to work on it tomorrow either," Evie pointed out. "We've got band practice after school."

"We'll come after school on Tuesday then," said Florence.

"Let's go to the den now," suggested Natalie, shaking raindrops from her prickles. "We can take the sail with us and mend it there."

Florence tucked it under her arm, and they scampered to the den, keeping under wide leaves for shelter wherever they could.

"Thank goodness!" Honey cried, as they crawled in through the entrance and up the tunnel to their den. "I'm drenched."

They rubbed themselves dry with old leaves that had drifted inside, then Evie spread the striped picnic blanket on the floor, and Natalie arranged the cushions and beanbags.

"Who wants a carrot pasty?" Florence asked, flopping down on a beanbag.

"Me!" squeaked Honey.

They tucked in hungrily. "I'll bring my sewing kit on Tuesday so we can mend the sail," said Natalie. "But we'll need something to patch it with."

"I've got an old dress," said Evie.

"Perfect," said Florence. "Just think! Our very own boat!"

"Only until we find the owner," Natalie reminded her.

"I know," said Florence. "But until then, we'll make the most of it."

Chapter Three

Next afternoon, Mr Wintergreen arrived just before school ended. The friends exchanged excited smiles – band practice was about to start.

"Hello, everyone," said Mr Wintergreen.

"If you're not in the band, you may go home," said Mr Hazelgrove, their teacher, as he opened the cupboard and took out the music stands. "The rest of you, get out your instruments."

"I practised my singing last night," said Honey to her friends.

"Me, too," said Natalie, who was also singing in the band. "But not too much. I don't want to be picked for a solo!"

"That's something I don't need to worry about!" Evie giggled. "I sing like a crow. And there's not much practising needed with woodblocks." She took two, one large, one small, out of her bag.

Harvey and Albie barged past, carrying a drum each. "Gangway!" Harvey cried. "Drummers coming through!"

"Honestly, those two!" exclaimed Honey.

"It's a shame band practice is today," said Evie. "I really want to get working on the boat."

"We can start fixing it tomorrow," said Florence, opening her school bag to get out her flute. "That's weird," she said, puzzled. "My flute's not here."

"It's not like you to forget something," said Natalie.

"I didn't forget it," Florence said. "I definitely put it in here this morning." She delved right down to the bottom of the bag, but the flute wasn't there.

"Maybe it fell out," Evie suggested. She peered under the desks. "No, I can't see it."

"Rosie!" said Florence. "I left my bag in the hall while I went into the kitchen to get my packed lunch. I bet she took it out."

"What will you do?" asked Honey.

"I don't know. There's no time to run home and get it."

"Take one of my woodblocks," Evie suggested. "Then we can sit together."

"Thanks," said Florence, but she was bitterly disappointed. She'd been so looking forward to playing her flute in the band for the first time.

Mr Wintergreen clapped his paws. "Come and sit down. Singers at the front, please."

"See you later," squeaked Honey excitedly. "Come on, Nat!"

Florence and Evie sat with the other percussionists.

"The wind instruments should be over here, Florence," said Mr Wintergreen.

"I've … um … left my flute at home," Florence muttered, her ears drooping.

"Left it at home? What's the good of that?" scolded Mr Hazelgrove, eyeing her sternly. "Mr Wintergreen's given up his time to organize this band. The least you can do is remember to bring your flute to school on the right day."

"Sorry, sir."

Evie squeezed Florence's arm. "At least it gives you a bit longer to practise," she whispered. "By next week you'll be playing brilliantly."

Florence forced a smile. The way things were going with Rosie, she probably wouldn't be able to practise at all.

Mr Wintergreen waved his baton, and Florence and Evie tapped their woodblocks in time. Luke and Lily Willowherb played violins, Monty Hornbeam came in on his cello and Sophie Chervil tooted her oboe.

Bluebell Woods

Natalie and Honey stood up to sing, but before they could start, Harvey and Albie began rapping so loudly on the drums that the rest of the band was drowned out.

Mr Wintergreen lifted his paw, signalling them all to stop. "Not so loud, boys, please," he said to Harvey and Albie. He raised his baton. "Now from the beginning."

They went through the song several times. "It sounds really good, doesn't it?" whispered Evie to Florence, as they came to the end.

"Yes," Florence agreed. But she couldn't help thinking that perhaps it would have sounded even better if she'd been playing her flute.

Florence met her dad just as she reached home. "How was band practice?" he asked. "Did you show Mr Wintergreen your flute?"

"I didn't have it," Florence said quietly. "I think Rosie took it out of my bag. And Mr Hazelgrove told me off for forgetting it."

"Oh dear," said Dad. "That was naughty of Rosie to take it. The trouble is she's too young to understand that it's your flute, not hers."

"I know," Florence said. "But I've got to practise. Even if I take my flute into my bedroom, she comes in and looks at me with those sad eyes…"

Mr Candytuft laughed. "She does the same to me when I won't let her have another cookie!" He scratched his nose thoughtfully. "Leave it with me."

As they went into their burrow, Rosie came skipping along the hall, holding the flute. "Daddy!" she cried.

Putting down his sack of sheep's wool, Dad took the flute and handed it to Florence. Then he swung Rosie up in the air and turned her over. "How's my upside-down girl?" he asked.

Giggling, Rosie tweaked his nose.

Florence followed them into the kitchen where Mum was sewing.

"Florence, I'm sorry about your flute," she said. "I didn't realize Rosie had it until just now, otherwise I'd have brought it into school."

"Never mind. I played one of Evie's woodblocks instead," said Florence. "And I can practise my flute now if Dad keeps Rosie amused."

"Right you are," said Dad. "Practise away!"

Florence hurried into her bedroom, took out her music and began to play. This might be her only chance to practise all week, and she was going to make the most of it.

"Last one to the boat's a landlubber!" cried Evie on Tuesday afternoon after school, as the friends raced down to the boat. She was holding an old dress to patch the sail. Florence was carrying a bucket of red paint, Honey had brought brushes and Natalie had her sewing kit tucked under her arm.

"We'll have to turn the boat over to paint it," Natalie said. "I hope it's not too heavy."

"We managed to get it out of the water," Evie pointed out, "so turning it over should be easy-peasy."

To Florence's relief, the boat was still there, hidden beneath the willow tree.

They put everything down, then took the oars and mast out of the boat, and all stood on the same side.

"Ready, steady, push!" cried Honey. The boat tilted easily and, with another shove, rolled right over, settling upside down.

Evie tore a strip of rough bark off the willow tree and snapped it into four pieces. "Here," she said, handing them out. "Let's rub off the old paint."

They set to work eagerly, chattering about the fun they'd have when the boat was repaired.

"Let's give it a name," Honey suggested.

"It might already have one," said Florence. "There's something written at the front of the boat."

They all stopped working to have a look.

"Shame we didn't spot it before we turned the boat over," said Evie. "It's hard to read upside down."

"If we can work out what it says, it might help us find the owner," said Natalie. She bent over, trying to see better. "The letters are pretty faded, but I think it might say *Truly Truly*."

"That doesn't mean anything," said Florence.

"Well, it won't help us find the boat's owner," Natalie said. "*Truly Truly* could belong to anyone."

"Let's call it *The Pink Parasol* instead," suggested Honey.

Evie laughed. "Honey, the boat's going to be red, not pink. And it doesn't look a bit like a parasol."

"We could paint a picture of one on the side," Honey said hopefully.

"We're trying to make the boat look the same as it did before – only better – in case we find the owner," Evie reminded her. "They might not be too pleased to see a pink parasol on the side."

"Oh, but—"

"Shall we start?" suggested Natalie, handing out the paint brushes.

Florence and Natalie painted one side of the boat, while Honey and Evie did the other.

"There," Florence said when they'd

finally finished. They all stood back to admire their handiwork.

"It looks amazing," said Evie. "You'd never guess it was so tatty before."

"And it's much better than Harvey and Albie's mouldy old raft," Honey added.

"Shame we have to leave it overnight for the paint to dry," said Florence.

"Why don't we go to the den and mend the sail?" said Natalie. "Then everything will be ready by the time we finish school tomorrow."

Tomorrow we'll be able to take the boat out on the river, Florence thought excitedly. She could hardly wait!

Chapter Four

Florence gazed gloomily out of the window next morning as she ate her breakfast. Rain was pattering against the glass and the branches of the crab-apple tree were tossing in the wind.

"Bother!" she sighed. There was no way they'd be able to go sailing in weather like this.

It rained all day. And the next day, and the next...

"Oh, this is hopeless," groaned Honey, as the friends picked their way between the puddles on their way home from school on Friday. "We'll never get out in the boat if this rain keeps up!"

"Hopefully the weather will be better tomorrow," said Natalie. "We could have a whole day of boating if it is because there's no school."

"Yes, and don't forget Florence's picnic on Sunday!" Honey said.

Florence looked up at the heavy, grey clouds. Touching her tail three times for luck, she wished for a fine weekend.

"Let's meet up at the boat first thing," said Evie. "I'll get the sail from the den."

"Only if it's dry, though," Honey said. "If it's raining as hard as this, the boat will fill up with water before we've even pushed off from the bank!"

Florence had hoped to spend the evening practising her flute, but when she arrived home, Rosie was sitting on her bed, tooting away happily.

"Hello, Rosie." Florence fetched her little sister's spinning top. "Here," she said, setting it going. "Tops are much more fun than a flute."

Rosie ignored her big sister and carried on blowing the flute.

Mum came in. "Come with me, Rosie." Handing the flute to Florence, she scooped up Rosie.

Rosie burst into tears.

"Come on now!" Mum said. "Let's find you some toys to play with."

"It's OK," Florence said. She couldn't bear to see her little sister upset. "I'll practise some other time."

She handed Rosie the flute. *But I've got to find a way of practising,* she thought. *Otherwise Mr Wintergreen might not let me stay in the band.*

Sunlight was slanting across Florence's bedroom ceiling when she woke next morning. "Yippee!" she exclaimed, instantly wide awake. They'd be able to spend the whole day out on the river.

She threw on her clothes and raced into the kitchen. Mum and Dad were sitting at the table, sipping mugs of dandelion tea.

"You're up early, darling," said Mum.

"I'm meeting Evie, Nat and Honey," Florence explained.

Dad ladled porridge into a bowl and set it in front of Florence. "Where are you four off to today?"

Bluebell Woods

"Er … Bluebell Woods," said Florence. She didn't mention the boat in case Mum and Dad said she couldn't go. "And tomorrow we'd like to have a picnic for my birthday on Midsummer Island. Natalie's offered to make it."

"You can never have too many picnics, in my opinion!" Dad said.

Florence gobbled her breakfast, then jumped up. "I'm off. I probably won't be back for lunch."

"Take these, then." Mum wrapped some walnut bars in a cloth and handed them to Florence. "I don't want you all going hungry."

"Thanks." Florence kissed her mum and dad, and hurried out of the door. She tore down to the boat, where Evie, Natalie and Honey were already waiting.

"I've brought the sail," Evie said.

"Let's get the boat in the water then!" cried Honey, jigging on the spot excitedly.

"How about launching it over there away from the reeds," said Florence, "where the bank slopes down to the water?"

"Hang on," Natalie said. "I've brought a brush and some waterproof ink so we can paint on the boat's name. Let's turn it over."

They rolled the boat over and Honey, who had the neatest handwriting, painted *Truly Truly* near the front where the old name had been.

"We still have to fit the mast, too," said Evie.

Together they lifted it up and fitted it into the socket in the bottom of the boat. "It doesn't lean at all now," said Florence approvingly.

With everyone pushing together, they slid the boat out from under the willow branches, and sent it gliding down the slope into the water. It landed with a gentle splash that sent ripples scudding across the brook.

"Hurray!" they all cheered.

"Who's going to row us away from the bank?" asked Honey, as she scrambled aboard, setting the boat rocking.

"I will," said Florence eagerly. None of them had ever rowed a boat before, but she was sure it couldn't be too difficult. She passed the oars to Honey, who laid them along the middle of the boat.

Bluebell Woods

"And me," Evie said. "One oar each, Florence."

"And I'll steer," volunteered Natalie.

"Here's the sail," said Evie, handing it to Honey. "We'll put it up when we get into the middle of the brook away from the bank."

Florence climbed into the boat. Sitting down on the middle seat, she reached out to Evie.

"Thanks," Evie said, taking Florence's paw to steady herself.

Natalie climbed in last and sat in the stern by the tiller.

"Our very own boat," said Honey.

"Until we find the owner," Natalie reminded her.

"But it's still ours for now," Honey said.

Florence and Evie fitted the oars into the rowlocks, and Natalie pushed off from the shore.

"My feet are getting wet," Honey said, puzzled.

"So are mine," said Florence. Looking down, she saw that the boat was filling up with water. "We're sinking!" shrieked Evie.

Chapter Five

Honey leaped up, making the boat tilt
dangerously. "Help!"

"Sit down, Honey!" shouted Evie.
"You'll tip us over and I can hardly swim!"

Cupping their paws together, they
began frantically bailing out the water.

"Faster!" yelled Evie.

"Calm down, girls," called a deep voice.

Looking up, Florence saw Mr
Willowherb, the ferryman, on the bank.
He waded into the water and dragged the
boat to the shore.

"There you go," he said, helping them climb out one by one.

"Thanks, Mr Willowherb," they said gratefully.

"You saved us from drowning!" added Honey.

"The water's only knee-deep here, Honey," said Mr Willowherb, laughing.

He hauled the boat out of the water and turned it over. "There's the trouble," he said, pointing to a small hole in the hull. "That needs filling. And then the whole boat could do with a coat of varnish to keep the wet out. I'll go and fetch some while you're mending the hole." He set off along the bank.

"What shall we mend it with?" asked Florence.

"Bark," said Evie, climbing the willow tree. She gnawed off a strip of bark and dropped it down to them.

Honey and Natalie tore it into tiny pieces, and Florence stuffed it into the hole. "That should do it," she said. "And the varnish will seal it so no more water can get in."

Mr Willowherb was soon back with a pot of varnish and four brushes. "Would you like me to ask Luke and Lily to give you a sailing lesson?" he said. "They've got their own little boat and they're always out on the river."

"Yes, please!" cried Florence.

"First thing tomorrow?" he asked. "The varnish will be dry by then."

"Perfect," said Evie. "Thanks, Mr Willowherb."

As soon as he'd gone, they set to work varnishing the boat. "You know we planned to have my birthday picnic tomorrow?" Florence said. "Let's not go to Midsummer Island. Let's go out in the boat and find a new picnic spot instead."

"Brilliant idea!" the others cried.

Luckily, the next day was bright and sunny, too. Luke and Lily Willowherb were already waiting by the willow tree when the friends arrived.

"What a lovely boat!" said Lily.

"Thanks," said Honey, helping Natalie place the picnic basket in the boat.

"Come on, let's get you launched," said Luke.

They pushed the boat into the brook, then climbed in. Honey stowed the picnic basket under the front seat. It was very crowded with all six of them in the boat but, to everyone's relief, no water came in.

"First I'll show you how to row," said Lily, sitting on the middle seat. "Sit next to me, Florence, and grab an oar."

Lily showed them how to row, dipping her oar into the water and pulling back. "Then lift it clear of the water, push forward and dip again," she said.

Florence followed her instructions and soon the boat was scudding along the brook. "It's not difficult at all," she said happily. "Who wants a go now?"

When they'd all got the hang of rowing, Luke showed them how to raise and lower the sail. "Lowering it a bit lets you slow down," he explained. "Because a smaller sail catches less wind." He let them all have a turn.

"It's the perfect day for sailing," Lily said. "A bit of a breeze, but not too much."

"But the boat doesn't stop straight away when we lower the sail," said Evie. "Does that mean we're doing it wrong?"

"No. The boat keeps drifting, depending on how fast you're going," explained Luke. "But it will slow down."

"Though if you head downstream the current will carry the boat along, too," Lily added.

"Sailing's trickier than rowing," said Honey.

"It is," Lily agreed. "And the trickiest thing of all is tacking."

"What's that?" asked Natalie.

"It's sailing a zigzag course so you can travel into the wind," said Lily. "But maybe that's a bit advanced for a first lesson. Why don't you row back today and we'll teach you how to tack another time?"

"How far will we be able to go?" asked Florence. "Have you been to either end of the Babbling Brook?"

"No, it goes on for miles in both directions," said Lily.

She and Luke slipped over the side of the boat into the water. "We'll swim along with you for a bit," she said, "to make sure you're OK."

Evie raised the sail. It billowed out and the *Truly Truly* surged forward. Florence sat by the tiller and steered a straight course downstream, keeping them out in the middle of the brook away from the shallow water near the banks.

"That's right," Lily called. "You won't get grounded if you stay in the deeper water."

They sailed on to a bend in the brook. "You seem to have got the hang of it so we'll head back now," said Lily. "Have a good trip."

"Thanks for showing us what to do," Natalie said.

"Yes, thanks," the others called. "Goodbye."

Florence pulled on the tiller and they all waved until the boat rounded the corner and the two otters were out of sight.

"Here goes then," said Florence. "Our very first voyage."

Chapter Six

"Bluebell Woods looks different from here," said Natalie, as they skimmed over the sparkling water. The banks were cloaked in yellow celandines, like tiny suns.

"Look," said Evie, pointing. "That's where we found loads of mushrooms. And there's the tree I climbed when me and Florence got lost in the woods."

A kingfisher flew across in front of them in a flash of vivid blue.

"I wish we could go on sailing for ever," Florence sighed happily.

The brook grew wider as they sped along. "It's turned into a river," said Honey.

"Oh," said Natalie, as they came across some tadpoles darting about in search of food. "Let's stop a moment and watch them." She dipped her paw in the water and the tadpoles swam over to investigate.

Evie lowered the sail and the boat slowed until it was drifting lazily.

An old heron flew down, his wing beats stirring the water into ripples. Landing in the shallows close to the bank, he folded his enormous grey wings.

"Hello," he said, stretching his long neck and peering short-sightedly at them. "Lovely day for a river trip!"

"It is," agreed Honey. "I'm Honey, and these are my friends Florence, Natalie and Evie. We're going on a picnic."

"My name's Ferdinand Fisher and I'm very pleased to make your acquaintance." The heron nodded enthusiastically, setting the long, black feathers on top of his head waggling. "I recognize that boat," he said suddenly.

Florence's heart sank. "Do you know who owns it?" she asked.

Lifting one foot, the heron scratched his tummy thoughtfully. "Two rabbits," he said, at last.

"Do you know where they live, Mr Fisher?" asked Evie sadly.

Mr Fisher frowned. "Sorry, I can't remember. It's years since I last saw them."

The friends exchanged hopeful glances. Perhaps the owners had moved away from Bluebell Woods and they'd be able to keep the boat after all.

"Anyway, if you're looking for a picnic spot," said Mr Fisher, "there's a nice sandy place a little further on."

"We'll look out for it," Florence said. "Thank you!"

The friends hoisted the sail again and cruised on. As they rounded the next bend, Florence spotted a gently sloping, sandy shore. "Over there!" she cried, swinging the tiller round. "I bet that's where Mr Fisher meant."

Jumping up eagerly, Honey loosened the ivy stem rope that secured the sail. "I can't hold it!" she squeaked. The sail flopped down on top of them all, and there was the sound of sploshing water as the boat rocked wildly from side to side.

Florence struggled out from underneath the sail, giggling. As she lifted one corner to help the others out, she heard a shout.

"Help!"

Spinning round, she saw that Evie had

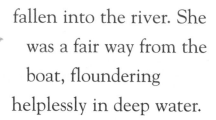 fallen into the river. She was a fair way from the boat, floundering helplessly in deep water.

"Help!" she screamed. "I'm sinking!"

"I'm coming, Evie," Florence called, leaping into the water. She swam faster than she'd ever swum before, her legs and arms pumping hard. The water was cold and she couldn't reach the bottom, but she was a strong swimmer.

She soon reached Evie and grabbed

her round the chest. "I've got you," she panted. "Keep still and I'll tow you back to the boat."

"Thanks, Florence," said Evie through chattering teeth. "The sail knocked me overboard."

As Florence turned in the water, she saw that Natalie and Honey had freed themselves from the sail and were rowing in their direction. Keeping a tight hold on Evie, she swam towards the boat.

As she drew near, Honey reached out with her oar. "Grab hold," she cried.

Gratefully, Florence and Evie caught hold of the oar, and Honey and Natalie pulled them over to the boat. They scrambled aboard, shivering.

"Thanks, Florence. It's lucky you're such a good swimmer," said Evie. She wrung out her dripping dress. "That was scary."

"I'm sorry about the sail," said Honey. "The rope slipped through my paws."

"Never mind that now," Natalie said. "Let's row ashore and light a fire so Florence and Evie can get dry. They look frozen."

"The water's not exactly warm," Florence said. "A fire sounds perfect."

Natalie and Honey rowed to the bank and they all scrambled out of the boat.

"I'm drying off already," said Evie, as they scurried to and fro in the sunshine, collecting wood.

Natalie then found two flint stones and struck them together to make a spark to light the fire.

Florence and Evie sat down beside it, holding out their paws to warm them, while Honey and Natalie set out the picnic.

"It's too hot by the fire for me," said Honey. "But I'm ready for lunch. Sailing's made me hungry."

They eagerly tucked into the delicious chestnut tarts and chickweed salad that Natalie had brought.

"These are really yummy, Nat," said Florence, helping herself to another tart.

"Wait till you taste the blossom cakes," Natalie said, unwrapping them.

By the time they'd finished their picnic, Florence and Evie were warm and dry again. Natalie poured a mug of river water on the fire to put it out, then they climbed back into the boat and pushed off from the bank. Evie hoisted the sail and soon they were bowling along once more.

"There's a bend ahead," said Natalie, who was sitting in the front.

Florence was steering. "Thanks, Nat," she said. "It's handy having a lookout."

As they rounded the bend, Natalie

gasped in dismay. "Watch out!" she called.
An enormous barge was moored directly
in their path.

Florence pushed the tiller over as hard
as she could, but there was no way of
avoiding the barge. "Hold on tight!" she
cried, as they crashed into the back of it
with a bump that sent them all tumbling
out of their seats.

"Is everyone all right?" Evie asked.

"I am," said Florence, clambering back
on to her seat.

"Me, too," said Natalie and Honey.

Just then a water vole, who looked
about the same age as them, appeared on
the deck of the barge. "Hey, look where
you're going!" he shouted.

"It's your fault we crashed," retorted
Evie. "You shouldn't be moored on a bend."

"My fault?" the water vole yelled.

"Sorry," Natalie called, trying to keep
the peace. At least there didn't seem to be
any damage to the barge. "Let's get
moving," she said in a low voice. She
hated rows and the water vole looked
angry enough to keep arguing all day.

Evie and Honey pushed the *Truly Truly*
away from the barge with an oar, then the
sail filled with wind and they were off again.

They sped past the barge and on along
the river.

"Hey, the river splits up ahead," the vole called after them. "Take the left fork."

"It's not far now," said Natalie. "Get ready to turn left, Florence."

"No, wait!" Evie cried. "That bit of the river's narrow and overgrown. He might be playing a trick on us. Go right, Florence."

Florence looked along the river's left fork. A narrow channel of water wound between beds of reeds under branches so low that they'd have to duck to get along. "I think Evie's right," she said. "We'll probably get stuck if we go down there."

They swung right and sailed on.

"The water vole's coming after us," said Honey. Sure enough, the barge was racing after them, sending wide waves sweeping across the river to the banks on either side.

"Can we go any faster?" asked Florence.

"No, the sail's as high as it will go," Honey said.

"What's that?" Natalie asked, pointing ahead. Something was jutting up out of the water.

"It's a rock," said Florence.

"Let's lower the sail a bit," said Evie, untying the rope. "We need to slow down so we can steer round it."

"What about the barge, though?" asked Natalie uneasily. It was closer than ever now and they could see the water vole at the front, waving his arms furiously.

"Come back!" he yelled over the roar of the engine.

"Just ignore him," Evie said. She lowered the sail a little, but the boat didn't slow down.

"Why aren't we going slower?" cried
Honey.

Evie brought the sail right down.
"That should do the trick."

But the boat only sped up, the water
splashing against its sides.

"The water's moving faster here," Honey
gasped. "And we're caught in the current."

They were racing towards the rock, and
Florence could see more rocks up ahead.
"Hold tight!" she cried. "We're heading
towards some rapids and we can't stop!"

Chapter Seven

Florence swung the tiller round, desperate to reach the bank, but the boat kept racing onwards.

"What are we going to do?" Honey cried. "Our boat will be smashed to pieces!"

"Catch!" cried a voice behind them.

Turning, the friends saw that the barge had almost caught them up. The young water vole was leaning out with a coiled rope in his paw; one end was fastened to the barge. He threw the rope and it snaked towards them, uncoiling in midair.

Florence caught it and tied it round the middle seat.

The barge's engine roared, then their headlong rush slowed as it began to move backwards, towing them away from the rapids.

"Thank goodness," Florence sighed.

When they were safely away from the rocks, the barge pulled them to the shore.

The friends climbed out on to the bank shakily. "That was close," gasped Natalie, squeezing Florence's paw.

The water vole jumped down from the barge. "Are you all OK?" he asked.

"Yes," said Florence. "Thanks for saving us. We should have listened to your advice."

"No problem." He grinned at them. "My name's Ralph Reedmace."

"Sorry we bumped into you," said Evie.

"I'm Evie Morningdew…"

The friends introduced themselves.

"Good to meet you," Ralph said.
"Sorry I shouted at you. Do you want to come aboard and look round our home?"

"You live on this barge?" asked Honey.

"Yes," said Ralph.

Eagerly, the friends climbed aboard and found themselves on a small deck made of polished wood. A young female water vole, who looked about the same age as Evie's little brother Reggie, was sitting beside the tiller.

"This is my sister, Poppy," said Ralph.

Poppy was wearing a straw hat with purple ribbons and two white feathers.

"Isn't that your hat, Florence?" Honey whispered, surprised.

Florence nodded, equally confused.

"Hello," Poppy said. "I steered the barge when Ralph was rescuing you. It was really heavy, but I managed it all by myself." She smiled proudly. "You're looking at my Present-from-the-River hat," she said, turning to Honey and Florence.

The friends exchanged awkward glances.

"Don't you like it?" asked Poppy, her face falling.

"It's lovely," said Florence. She didn't have the heart to tell Poppy that it was her lost birthday hat.

"It's Florence's hat!" Honey burst out.

"Oh! I thought the river gave it to me." Poppy's eyes filled with tears, as she held out the hat to Florence.

"It's OK," said Florence. "You can keep it, Poppy. You helped rescue us, after all. It really suits you." Florence was sure Granny and Grandpa wouldn't mind too much.

"Can I really keep it? Thank you!" Poppy exclaimed. "Shall I go and get Mum and Dad so we can tow your boat home for you?"

"Yes, please," said Evie quickly. "It's getting late and it's a long way to row."

Poppy jumped off the barge and scampered away into the woods.

"Come inside," said Ralph. They followed him through a low door and down some steps into a narrow, low-ceilinged living room. A red sofa and two matching armchairs stood by a stove with a crooked chimney. Shiny pots and pans hung beside the stove and colourful plates were arranged on a nearby row of shelves.

"What a cosy room!" exclaimed Florence. "It must be brilliant to live on a boat!"

"I'll show you the cabins," said Ralph. They followed him across the living room, walking one behind the other because it was so narrow. A door at the far end led into an even narrower corridor.

"I share this room with Poppy," said
Ralph, showing them a tiny cabin with
bunk beds and a round window. "I sleep in
the top one and Poppy sleeps underneath."

"Where do you keep all your things?"
asked Florence.

Ralph pointed out two built-in
cupboards below the lowest bunk.

"The ceiling's very low," Evie said. "Do you ever bang your head when you sit up in bed?"

Ralph laughed. "I used to, but not any more. You soon learn to be careful."

The next room was Ralph's parents' cabin, with a double bed covered in a bright patchwork quilt.

"You'd never think you could fit so many rooms into such a small space," Honey said, amazed. She pointed to a door at the far end of the corridor. "What's in there?"

"The engine room," said Ralph.

Peeping in, they saw baskets of wood piled along one wall. In the middle of the room was the engine, a huge thing with arms and levers that rattled and pumped noisily. Beside it was the furnace that burned the wood and powered the engine.

"It's boiling in here," Natalie said, fanning her face with her paw.

"Yes, but it's great in winter," Ralph said.

"Do you travel all the time?" asked Florence. She loved the idea of cruising along the river in her own little home.

"Yes," Ralph replied. "We're always on the move."

"So you and Poppy don't go to school?" Honey said.

"No, we have lessons at home from Mum and Dad." They heard footsteps overhead. "That'll be them now," said Ralph. "Come and say hello." He led the way back along the corridor and into the living room. Mr and Mrs Reedmace were coming down the stairs with Poppy. Mr Reedmace was a tall water vole with a whiskery face and bright eyes. His wife wore a flowery dress with a very full skirt. Florence wondered if it kept snagging on the furniture as she squeezed through the barge's narrow rooms.

"Hello," said Mrs Reedmace, beaming at them. "Poppy told us we had visitors."

Bluebell Woods

Ralph introduced them and explained what had happened.

"Where do you live, girls?" asked Mrs Reedmace.

"Bluebell Woods," said Evie. "Near the Stepping Stones."

"I know it," Mr Reedmace said. "We're going upstream anyway. I'll turn the barge round, then we'll be off. It's getting late."

"Let's go up top," suggested Ralph.

"Not you, Poppy," said Mrs Reedmace. "It's time to get ready for bed."

"Oh, Mum!" sighed Poppy. She squeezed past everyone, heading for her bedroom. "Goodnight," she said sadly.

"Goodnight, Poppy," the friends chorused. "Thanks for rescuing us."

They followed Ralph up the stairs, then clambered right up on to the barge's roof. The sun was low, its light slanting through the trees, casting long shadows and dappling the river with flecks of gold.

Mr Reedmace revved the engine.

"Here we go!" cried Honey. "What a brilliant way to get home!"

Chapter Eight

"Do you know how to make reed pipes?" asked Ralph, as the barge backed slowly across the river to turn round. Leaning over the side, he snapped off five thick reeds.

"No," said Natalie. "But we'd love to learn."

Ralph produced a penknife from his pocket and cut the reeds so they were all the same length. Then he showed them how to make finger holes and another, bigger mouth hole. "You blow across that

hole to make the notes," he said. He
played a cheerful tune on his pipe.

The friends took turns with his knife,
cutting out the holes carefully. Soon they
were all tooting their reed pipes.

"Can you teach us that tune you just
played, please, Ralph?"
asked Florence.

He showed them the
notes and before long they
were all playing together.

The sun slipped lower and a vivid,
orangey-red glow spread across the sky and
the river. Glancing back the way they'd
come, Florence saw that night was
creeping in behind them, sending streaks
of darkness across the sky. A few bats
skimmed overhead and birds flew by,
heading for their nests.

Softly, she began to play the tune she'd been trying to practise for the school band. Suddenly, she broke off. "I've had an idea!" she exclaimed. "I'll give my reed pipe to Rosie. Then, maybe, I'll get my birthday flute back."

"Good idea," chorused her friends.

"We're almost at the Stepping Stones," Mr Reedmace called.

"Gosh, that was quick," said Evie.

"Look, there's the willow tree!" cried Honey. "Can you let us off there, please, Mr Reedmace?"

Mr Reedmace steered the barge towards the tree and Ralph grabbed a mooring rope, ready to jump ashore.

"We'll have to start searching for the *Truly Truly*'s owner tomorrow," sighed Natalie.

"I wish we didn't have to," Honey huffed. "I love having a boat, even if we did nearly go over some rapids."

"Me, too," agreed Florence. "But Nat's right. It's not ours to keep," she added sadly.

"Look, there's your mum, Florence!" cried Evie, as the barge nosed in towards the bank. Mrs Candytuft was standing near the willow tree watching.

"Rosie's there, too," said Florence, surprised to see them. "And she's got my flute!"

Ralph leaped ashore and tied the rope to the willow tree's trunk, bringing the barge to a stop. Florence jumped down on to the bank.

"Are you all OK?" Mum asked. "You were out so late that I went looking for you. Mr Willowherb told me you'd gone sailing instead of visiting Midsummer Island."

"We're fine," said Florence. "Sorry if you were worried, Mum." She crouched down to speak to Rosie. "This is for you, Rosie," she said, holding out the reed pipe.

Rosie's face lit up. "My own flute!" she exclaimed, grabbing the reed pipe and letting Florence's flute drop to the ground.

Florence picked it up and beamed at Evie, Natalie and Honey as they jumped down from the barge. "I don't think I'll have trouble practising for the band any more," she said happily.

"Give us a hand to pull our boat in, Florence," said Evie. "Ralph's mum and dad probably want to get going."

They untied the *Truly Truly* from the barge, then pulled it in to the bank. "Bye. Thanks for everything," they called to Ralph, who was watching from the roof of the barge.

"Might see you again one day," Ralph called back, as the barge chugged away from the bank, heading towards Brook Deeps. "We come through Bluebell Woods now and then so I'll look out for you next time."

"Mind you do!" Florence cried.

Mrs Candytuft came over to look at the sailing boat as they tied it to a sturdy bramble. "Well, I never!" she gasped. "I know that boat!"

Florence's heart sank. If her mum knew who owned it they'd have no choice but to give it back.

"It belonged to your dad and me," Mrs Candytuft said, with a smile.

"Really?" cried Evie, astonished.

"Yes. I lived in Bramble Bank, a village a little way upstream, when I was young, and Florence's dad used to sail up to see me every day. We were always out and about on the river."

"So how did it end up here?" Florence asked.

"We lost it one night in a storm, just after we were married. We searched all along the river, but we never found it. Where was it?"

"Under this willow tree," said Honey. "And we mended a hole, painted and varnished it, and patched the sail."

"Is it called the *Truly Truly?*" asked Natalie. "The name was a bit rubbed off, but we thought that was what it said."

"*Truly* **Trudy**," said Mrs Candytuft.

"Trudy's your name," Florence said.

"It is," agreed her mum.

"So if we'd been able to read the name, we'd have known it belonged to you," Natalie said.

"I suppose you would. I think Florence's dad called the boat that to impress me," Mrs Candytuft said, laughing.

"It must have worked," said Honey, "because you married him."

"We should change the name," said Natalie. "It won't be difficult to turn an 'l' into a 'd'."

"Do you want your boat back, Mum?" asked Florence, hoping she'd say no. She wanted to go on lots more sailing trips with her friends.

"You girls can keep it," Mrs Candytuft replied. "You've done an amazing job of doing it up – it looks better than ever. Your dad and I might want to borrow it occasionally, though."

"Brilliant!" squeaked Honey, seizing

Florence's paws and swinging her round. "Thanks, Mrs Candytuft!"

"Now, let's get you all home," said Mrs Candytuft.

As she followed her mum and Rosie, Florence began to play the tune Ralph had taught them. Evie, Natalie and Honey joined in on their reed pipes, and their music seemed to hover in the air around them, before drifting away along the Babbling Brook.